BERNARD WABER

You're a Little Kid With a Big Heart

Houghton Mifflin Company, Boston
1980

for SARA BETH

Library of Congress Cataloging in Publication Data

Waber, Bernard.
 You're a little kid with a big heart.

 SUMMARY: When she is granted her wish to be
a grownup, Octavia decides she'd rather be a little
girl.
 [1. Wishes – Fiction] I. Title.
PZ7.W113Yo   [E]   79-23893
ISBN 0-395-29163-1

Octavia Blisswink
was just minding her own business,
not bothering anybody . . .

when she came across a kite
trapped in the branches of a tree.
"Little girl! Little girl!" called the kite.
"Get me out of this tree and I will
grant you a magic wish."

Octavia climbed the tree
and brought the kite down.
"Thank you," said the kite.
"Now, you may make
your wish."

Octavia tried to think of a wish.

"I wish . . ." she began.

"Yes . . ." said the kite.

"I wish . . ."

"Yes, yes . . ." said the kite.

"I wish . . ."

"Yes, yes, yes . . ." said the kite.

Octavia was so surprised and so excited,
she couldn't think of a wish quickly enough.
So she wished a wish she remembered wishing
two days earlier when her mother refused to allow her
to watch *The Mighty Monster Show* on television.

"I wish I was old enough to decide for myself
what I want to do — or not do," said Octavia.

"Wish granted," said the kite.

In a wink, Octavia was fully grown.
"Oh, look at me!" she gasped. "Look at my
long arms! Look at my big hands!
Look at my clothes! My clothes have grown too!"
"You are now thirty-nine years old,"
announced the kite.
"Thirty-nine!" Octavia gasped again.
"I thought I'd throw in a few extra years
just for good measure," said the kite.
"Wasn't that sporting of me?
Well . . . good-bye," called the kite,
flying off into the wind.
"Happy adulthood!"

Octavia wasn't the least bit sure she liked
what had happened to her, but she decided to look
at the brighter side.
"Just think," she told herself, "I won't have
to practice piano, kiss relatives, run errands,
be told not to do this, not to do that."
The more she thought about it,
the more Octavia was happy to be grown up . . .

so happy, in fact, she skipped
all the way home.

But when she told her mother what had happened,
her mother wasn't at all happy.
"I want my little girl back!" she cried again and again.
"But I *am* back," said Octavia. "I'm just a bit
older, that's all."
"A bit!" Her mother burst into fresh tears.
"Oh, how will I ever explain why my own child
is seven years older than I am?"

And when he heard about it, Octavia's father
was just as unhappy.
"A chance of a lifetime and this is what you
wished for," he groaned. "Why couldn't you have
wished for something sensible, like . . . like . . .
a bigger apartment, or . . . or . . .
a new refrigerator?"
"Oh, what are we going to do?" Octavia's mother
wrung her hands.
"I'll call the police," said her father.
"It's too late for the police!" her mother
came close to shrieking.

Octavia was surprised at the difference
being a grownup made at dinner.
Suddenly, her mother wasn't reminding her
to eat all of her string beans.
And her father didn't say,
"Don't reach! Ask for things to be
passed to you."

And that night, for the very first time in her
entire life, Octavia's parents went to bed
earlier than she.
"I am not telling a thirty-nine-year-old person
when to go to bed," said her father.
"Good night," said her mother. "You may borrow
one of my nightgowns when you're ready for bed."
"Good night," said her father. "Don't forget
to turn off the lights."
"Aren't you going to kiss me good night?"
asked Octavia.
"Oh, of course, dear," said her mother.
They kissed Octavia good night.

Octavia stayed up and watched television.
First she watched the late show.
After that she watched the late, late show.
And after that she watched the late, late, late show.
And all the while she watched television, Octavia
ate and ate and ate.
First she ate three gigantic helpings of
pistachio-marshmallow ice cream.
And after that she ate two enormous bowls of
Krispie-Krunchie dry cereal.
And after that she ate a giant-size bag of Fritos.
By the time she had watched three television channels go
off the air, Octavia was so stuffed, and so bleary-eyed,
that she decided, at last, it was time for bed.

"Mother! Mother!" called Octavia
the following morning. "I'll be late for school."
Her mother rushed into the bedroom.
"School? Oh, but you won't be going back
to school, dear," said her mother. "A grownups'
school, perhaps — but not a school for children."
"Oh, yes," said Octavia, remembering her new age.
Octavia looked at the empty shelves in her bedroom.
"Where is my teddy bear?" she asked. "And where
are my games and puzzles and stuffed animals?
Where are my bunny pictures? And where is
my record player, and my beanbag clown,
and my rocking chair?"
"Oh, I removed all of those earlier, while you
were asleep," said her mother. "I'll bring
them back if you really think you want them, dear.
But I thought . . . well . . . at your age . . ."

"Oh, yes," said Octavia. "I suppose I won't be wanting them now — not anymore. Will I?"
"Well, I hardly think so, dear," said her mother.

That afternoon, Octavia told her friends Laurie
and Harriet all about it.

"Can you do anything you want to do?" they asked.

"Uh-huh," Octavia answered proudly.

"Anything?" they asked again.

"Anything," said Octavia.

"Oh, lucky, lucky you!" cried her friends.

Octavia, Laurie, and Harriet began to play.

Octavia was having so much fun, she almost
forgot she was grown up.
But she was reminded when Harriet and
Laurie began to whisper.
"Why are you whispering?" Octavia asked.
"We have decided not to play with you ever again,"
Harriet announced. "We have decided we will
only play with people our own age."
"Good-bye!" said Harriet.
"Good-bye!" said Laurie.

Just like that, Octavia was left alone.
"I know," she decided, "I'll play with Hermie.
Hermie always was my best friend."

Octavia waited for Hermie
to come out of his apartment.
"Pssssssst! Hermie!" she called to him.
"Yes, ma'am," said Hermie.
"Don't you recognize me?"
"Yes, ma'am. I think so, ma'am," said Hermie.
"It's me, Tavie. Tavie Blisswink. Apartment 2C.
Remember? Remember our club?"
"No, ma'am. I mean, yes, ma'am. I don't
know ma'am," said Hermie.

"Do you want to play catch or something, Hermie?" Octavia asked.

"No, ma'am," said Hermie.

"How about if we toss the Frisbee?"

"No, ma'am," said Hermie.

"Then how about coming over to my place? Do you want to come over to my place, Hermie?"

"I don't think so, ma'am."

"What do you feel like doing, Hermie? You must want to do something. Huh, Hermie?"

"I don't know, ma'am," said Hermie.

Octavia was exasperated.

"Now you stop calling me ma'am!" she exploded.

"Do you hear me, Hermie? Or I'll . . .
I'll twist your arm!"

Hermie was struck with terror.

Suddenly, he bolted down the stairs
and flew out of the apartment building.
And once again Octavia was alone.

Several dreadfully boring days later, Octavia
decided to talk matters over with her parents.
"I don't know what to do," she told them. "I am
thirty-nine-years-old and I don't know what to do."
"It's a problem," said her mother.
"Perhaps you should think of settling down,"
her father suggested.
"I am settled!" Octavia almost screamed.
"I mean, you know, find some kind of work."
"How about if I get married," said Octavia.
"Who would you marry?" asked her mother.
"I can marry Hermie."
"Hermie is only seven years old," said her mother.
"I'll wait," said Octavia. "I'll wait until Hermie grows up."
"And in the meantime?" said her father.
"In the meantime, do you know where I can go to
meet other thirty-nine-year-olds?"
"Perhaps if you found a job," her father suggested again.
"All right," said Octavia, "I'll look for a job."

The next day, Octavia awoke bright and early,
and set out to look for a job.

"What kind of work do you wish?" asked the woman
at the desk.

"I don't know," said Octavia. "I never worked before."

"You were needed at home?" said the woman.

"No," said Octavia, "I just never worked before."

The woman looked at Octavia. "What can you do?" she asked.

"I can spell," said Octavia. "I was the best speller
in my whole class. I can spell really big words.
Listen: Mississippi . . . capital M-i-s-s-i-s-s-i-p-p-i.
And do you know what else I can do? I can do
all kinds of puzzles, the harder the better. And
I love cutting out."

"Cutting out?" said the woman.

"Pictures," said Octavia. "My favorites
are horses."

Once more, the woman looked at Octavia.
"I see," she said at last. "Well, we don't, at the moment, have a job for someone with your uh . . . skills, but should something come up, we will certainly be in touch. Good-bye!" The woman smiled cheerily.
"Good-bye!" said Octavia.

Octavia went home to await a call to work.
One dreary, plodding day followed the next.
She passed much of the time looking out the window,
watching children at play.

Early one evening, when she knew the neighborhood
children were at home getting ready for bed,
Octavia wandered out to the empty playground behind
the apartment building.
She smiled sadly as she imagined the many good-night
hugs and kisses, and last calls for drinks
of water.
She pressed her cheek against the cool chain
of a swing.

Octavia sat down on the swing and slowly pushed away.
Soon she was flying back and forth.
The wind pressed deliciously against her face
and raced through her hair.
"Higher! Higher!" she sang.
"Up to the sky!
Through the clouds!
Touch the stars!
Dance on the moon!
Higher! Higher! Higher!"

Octavia would have swung
the night away were it not for
a sudden chill in the air
that somehow reminded her
she was no longer a child.
She allowed the swing to
slow down and stop.
And there Octavia sat,
longing, longing, longing
for her lost childhood.

Several days later,
Octavia was at the window again,
enjoying the spectacle of
children gathered around
an ice cream truck,
when suddenly she noticed
something red bobbing merrily
in the wind.
She looked again.
Could it be?
It must be . . .
the magic kite.

Octavia burst out of the building,
racing after the kite.

She found it at last, and trapped again
in the very same tree.
"You! Kite! Give me back my childhood!
Do you hear me!" Octavia screamed.
"Who are you?" asked the kite.
"Octavia Blisswink. Remember?
I used to be seven years old."
"Ah, yes, it's coming back to me,"
said the kite. "That was many wishes ago,
and you wanted to be grown up."
"I've changed my mind," said Octavia.
"This is my thanks," the kite said wearily.
"I go around granting magic wishes, and
this is my thanks. If there is one kind
of person I can't abide,
it's the sore wisher."
"Never mind about that," said Octavia. "Now
you give me back my childhood! Immediately!
At once! Right now! Do you hear me, kite!
Or I'll . . . I'll . . .
rip you to shreds!"

"I don't know what it is about this tree,"
the kite sighed, "but if you will get me out of it,
I'll see what I can arrange."
Octavia took the kite down and held on to it
for dear life.
"You wouldn't care to settle for twenty years
of age, would you?" asked the kite.
"SEVEN!" Octavia shouted. "KITE, DO YOU HEAR ME?"
"Oh, very well," said the kite. "Reversing
a wish was never my style, but you rescued me;
therefore your wish is granted."

At once, Octavia was seven years old.
"Oh, thank you, thank you," she cried joyously,
all the while hugging and kissing the kite.
But the kite would have none of it.
"Just please let go of me," said the kite.
"I'm sorry," said Octavia, releasing it immediately.
"Well, happy childhood!" the kite called out in a
weary voice. "And, oh dear me, I do hope I remember to
stay out of your neighborhood."

Octavia ran back to her apartment.

"Mother! Mother!" she called.

"Look! I'm me again!"

"Oh, Octavia! Oh, my child,"
her mother sobbed.

That night, Octavia's parents tucked
her into bed.

"Look!" said her mother, "your teddy bear."

"Thank you," said Octavia. "And tomorrow
may I have my puzzles?"

"Oh, you certainly may," said her mother.

"And my games?"

"And your games."

"And my record player?"

"And your record player."

"And my beanbag clown?"

"And your beanbag clown."

"And my rocking chair?"

"And your rocking chair."

"And my bunny pictures?"

"And your bunny pictures."

"And my scissors?"

"And your scissors."

"And my Snoopy toothbrush?"

"And your Snoopy toothbrush."

"Do you want to know something?" said Octavia.
"I don't think I will ever want to grow up again."
"Ah, but you are mistaken," said her father.
"You most certainly will want to grow up.
In time you will be so happy . . .
and so ready to grow up.
In time, Octavia.
In dear . . . sweet . . .
oh, so precious, precious time."